SCOOBY-DOO!™

GIDDY UP, SCOOBY-DOO

Written by Lee Howard
Illustrated by Alcadia SNC

ABDO
Spotlight

ABDOPUBLISHING.COM

Reinforced library bound edition published in 2016 by Spotlight, a division of ABDO
PO Box 398166, Minneapolis, Minnesota 55439. Spotlight produces high-quality
reinforced library bound editions for schools and libraries. Published by agreement
with Warner Bros. Entertainment Inc.

Printed in the United States of America, North Mankato, Minnesota.
092015
012016

THIS BOOK CONTAINS
RECYCLED MATERIALS

CATALOGING-IN-PUBLICATION DATA

Howard, Lee.
 Giddy-up, Scooby-Doo / Lee Howard.
  p. cm. (Scooby-Doo leveled readers)
Summary: A mysterious horse thief is ruining all the fun at Tumbleweed Ranch. Shaggy and
Scooby saddle up to save the day.
1. Scooby-Doo (Fictitious character)--Juvenile fiction. 2. Dogs--Juvenile fiction. 3. Mystery and
detective stories--Juvenile fiction. 4. Adventure and adventures--Juvenile fiction.
[Fic]--dc23
            2015156075

978-1-61479-414-1   (Reinforced Library Bound Edition)

Spotlight
A Division of ABDO
abdopublishing.com

Scooby-Doo and the gang were spending a week at the Tumbleweed Ranch.

"Wow," said Shaggy. "This place is cool."

"Reah!" said Scooby.

The gang met Slim Jim the owner. "Welcome to Tumbleweed Ranch," he said.

"I'm sorry, but you came at a bad time," Slim Jim explained.

"Someone is stealing my best horses."

"Let us do some investigating," offered Fred.

"But we need a way to get close to the horses," said Fred.

"How about you take our rodeo clown class," said Slim Jim.

Shaggy and Scooby were naturals at playing the fool.

"You two will make perfect rodeo clowns!" said Jingles.

"Did you hear that, Scoob?" said Shaggy. "Like, we're gonna be clowns."

"Roh roy!" Scooby answered.

Their first lesson was in roping.
Shaggy roped Scooby!
Scooby roped Shaggy!

The rest of the gang watched their friends' antics.

"Jinkies!" said Velma. "What are those two doing?"

"Acting like clowns!" said Daphne.

After class, Slim Jim introduced the gang to a very tall cowboy.

"This is my neighbor Ray Bob Gilley," said Slim Jim.

"Howdy," said Ray Bob.
"He used to own this ranch and all the horses," said Slim Jim.

That night, the gang made a campfire.
They heard strange noises.
"What's that?" Velma asked.
"It sounds like some horses," Fred said.

The gang ran to the stables.

"Two more horses are gone," said Slim Jim sadly.

"Maybe the rustler left a clue," said Velma.

Looking around the stables, they found streaks of white goo on the ground. "What's this?" asked Daphne.

"White clown make-up," said Fred. "And yarn!"
"Someone's been clowning around in here,"
said Velma.

The next day, Jingles taught Scooby and Shaggy how to juggle.
Or at least, he tried to teach them.

After class, Fred and Daphne followed Jingles to the stables.

Jingles patted one of the horses.

"See you later, Blackie," he whispered.

Fred and Daphne quickly hurried back to the gang.

Shaggy and Scooby were toasting marshmallows with Velma.

"We need to catch this horse thief in the act," said Fred.

"Like, how?" asked Shaggy.

"We'll camp out at the stables tonight," said Daphne.

Later, the gang went to their tents to wait. Soon, Shaggy and Scooby were sound asleep. Suddenly, a big, scary shadow appeared outside their tent.

"AHHHHHH!" Shaggy cried, waking up. Shaggy and Scooby slid deep inside their sleeping bags.

"Get your lasso Scoob, it's time for a little rope practice," Shaggy said.

Outside, Scooby and Shaggy could see a dark figure leading a horse away from the stables.

Scooby threw his lasso into the shadows and amazingly enough, he caught something.

"Ree-ha!" Scooby shouted.

With all the noise, Fred, Daphne, and Velma came running with Jingles and Slim Jim not far behind.

"We caught the horse thief!" Shaggy cried.

"I guess I taught you something right," Jingles grinned.

"If it's not Jingles, who is it?" asked Fred.

"Let's see," said Daphne.

She revealed the thief's face with a flashlight.

"Ray Bob Gilley!" the gang shouted.

Ray Bob was taken to the Sherriff's station. "I was stealing back all the horses I had to sell," said Ray Bob.

"You pretended to be me," said Jingles. "So I'd get the blame."

"Looks like Ray Bob will be clowning around in jail," said Velma.

"Thanks to you meddling kids!" yelled Ray Bob.

The next day, the gang enjoyed their last barbecue.

"Anyone want to help me round up some prairie dogs?" asked Jingles.

"No, thanks," said Shaggy. "We're more interested in rounding up hot dogs!"

"Rup!" Scooby cried. "Scooby-Dooby-Doo!"